I'm The Bus Driver

Bus drivers have a very important job.
They drive passengers safely from place to place.
Now it's your turn to be the driver!

illustrated by **David Semple**

TICKETS

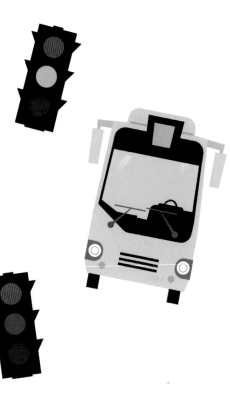

OXFORD
UNIVERSITY PRESS

Great Clarendon Street, Oxford OX2 6DP
Oxford University Press is a department of the University of Oxford.
It furthers the University's objective of excellence in research, scholarship,
and education by publishing worldwide. Oxford is a registered trade mark of
Oxford University Press in the UK and in certain other countries

Text copyright © Oxford University Press 2022
Illustrations © David Semple 2022
Text written by Katie Woolley

The moral rights of the author and illustrator have been asserted
Database right Oxford University Press (maker)

First published 2022

British Library Cataloguing in Publication Data

Data available
ISBN: 978-0-19-277774-4

1 3 5 7 9 10 8 6 4 2

Printed in China

Paper used in the production of this book is a natural,
recyclable product made from wood grown in sustainable forests.
The manufacturing process conforms to the environmental
regulations of the country of origin.

My name is

_____

and today I'm the
bus driver!

Today your job is to drive the bus through town
to take this family where they need to go.
School starts at 9 o'clock and the children
can't be late!

First you need to put on your uniform.
What do you need to be a bus driver?

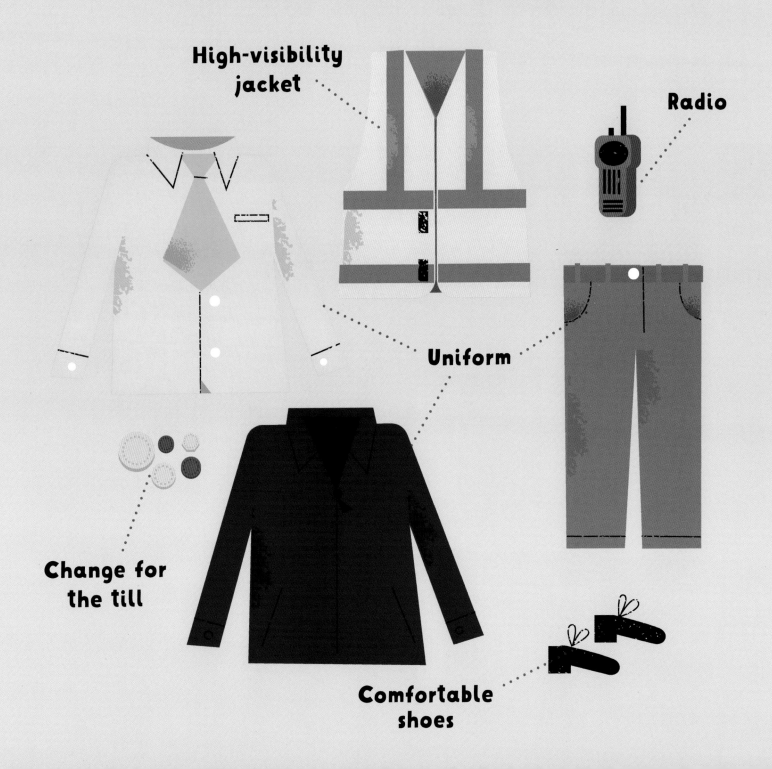

High-visibility
jacket

Radio

Uniform

Change for
the till

Comfortable
shoes

There are lots of buses at the bus depot.
You are driving bus number 4.
What colour is your bus?
What other colours can you see?

This is your bus!
Can you name all the parts?

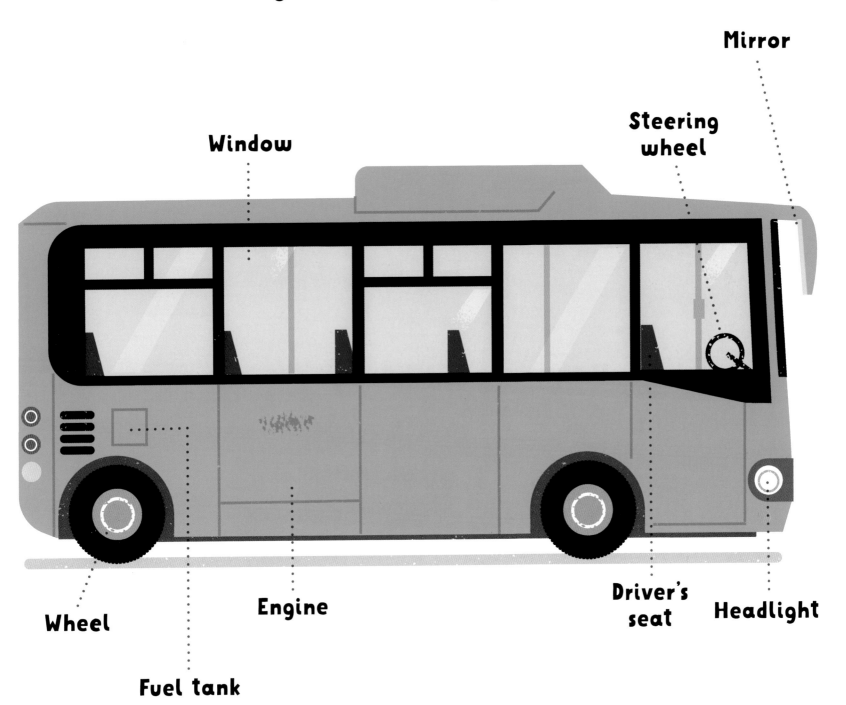

Mirror

Steering wheel

Window

Wheel

Fuel tank

Engine

Driver's seat

Headlight

It's 8 o'clock. Time to go!

Bell

Lever

To start
and stop
the engine

Horn

Speed
dial

START/
STOP

10   15

5   20

25

Put on your seatbelt, and check
your controls are working.
Wave goodbye to the other bus drivers.

BRRM BRRM!
Push the green button to start the engine.

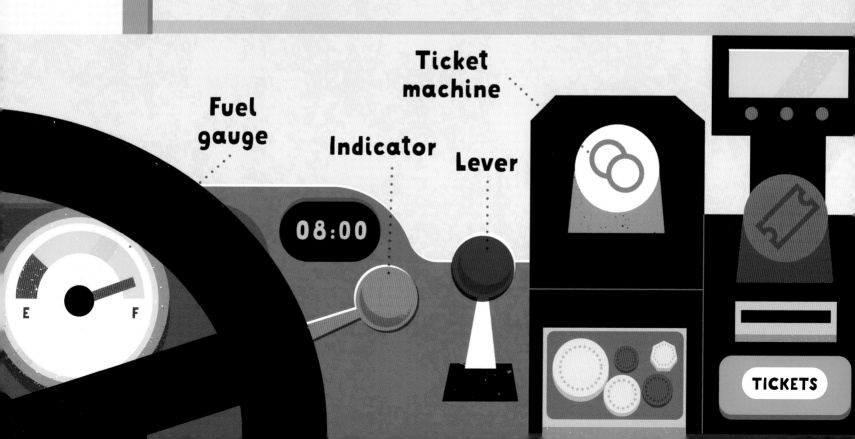

Ticket
machine

Fuel
gauge

Indicator

Lever

E F

08:00

TICKETS

The family are waiting at the bus stop.
The bus is right on time. Well done!

Stop the bus and pull the yellow lever to open the doors. Push the white button on your ticket machine five times and count out five tickets.

Oh no! It's starting to rain. You need to clear your windscreen. Pull the blue lever to start the windscreen wipers. That's better!

Windscreen wiper

SWISH SWISH!

START/ STOP

10 15 5 20 0 25

There are more passengers to pick up.
Stop the bus using the green button.
Then pull the yellow lever to open the doors.
Call out, "All aboard!"

SPLISH!
SPLASH!
SPLOSH!

08:10

E   F

TICKETS

This passenger is paying his fare with coins.
Check you have some change.
He needs 3 silver coins from your till.

The bus is full of passengers with places to be.
It's half past 8. School starts in half an hour.
Will you get the children to school on time?

Ambulance

Car

START/
STOP

The traffic lights are red.
Press the green button to stop the bus.
Count four vehicles up ahead. Can you name them all?

Dad's pushed the bell. He's off to the shops to buy six oranges and three slices of watermelon. Help him count them out. What shape are they?

Wave goodbye to Dad and push the green button to start the bus. Off we go!

There's just one more stop to go.
Which way to the school? Point left or right.
Where would the other way take you?

Push your orange indicator to signal the way to school.
Then turn the wheel to steer the bus.

AIRPORT

08:50

TIC
TIC
TIC!

TICKETS

Hurray! You've reached your final stop.
It's 9 o'clock and the children are
on time for school. Well done!

BEEP
BEEP!

START/
STOP

Everybody gives you a big cheer.
Join in and beep your horn to wish them a good day.

You're back at the bus depot, and there's one last thing to do. Can you guess what it is?

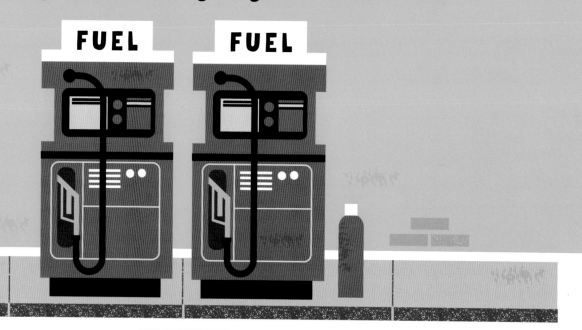

FUEL **FUEL**